6/14

Name:

Doctor:

First published by Walker Books Ltd.,
87 Vauxhall Walk, London SE11 5HJ

Copyright © 2007 by Lucy Cousins
Lucy Cousins font copyright © 2007 by Lucy Cousins

Maisy™. Maisy is a registered trademark of Walker Books Ltd., London.

First U.S. paperback edition 2009

Library of Congress Cataloging-in-Publication Data is available.

Library of Congress Catalog Card Number 2006049586

ISBN 978-0-7636-3377-6 (hardcover)
ISBN 978-0-7636-4372-0 (paperback)

18 19 APS 10 9 8 7 6 5

Printed in Humen, Dongguan, China

This book was typeset in Lucy Cousins.
The illustrations were done in gouache.

Candlewick Press
99 Dover Street
Somerville, Massachusetts 02144

visit us at www.candlewick.com

Maisy Goes
to the Hospital

Lucy Cousins

CANDLEWICK PRESS

One day, Maisy
was bouncing on
her trampoline.
She bounced
very high.

Oh, no!
Maisy fell.
She hurt her leg.

Poor Maisy!

Charley went with
Maisy to the hospital.

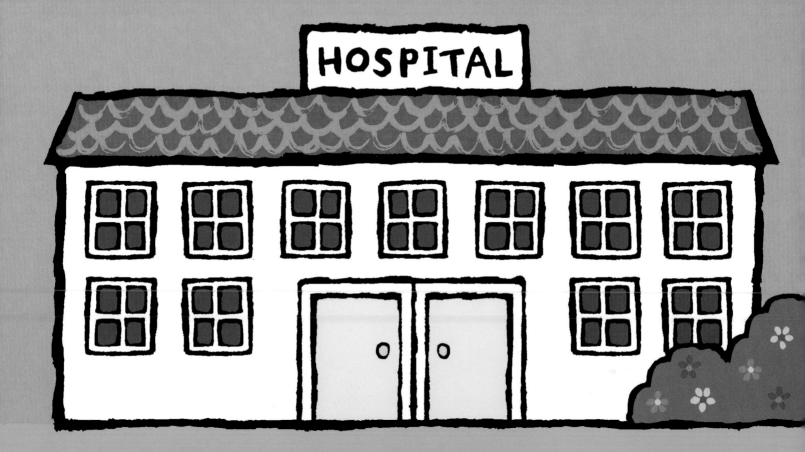

Maisy had never been
to the hospital before.

"You need to have an X-ray," Doctor Duck told Maisy.

The X-ray showed that Maisy had broken her leg.

Doctor Duck put a plaster cast on Maisy's leg.

Nurse Comfort put Maisy to bed in the children's ward.

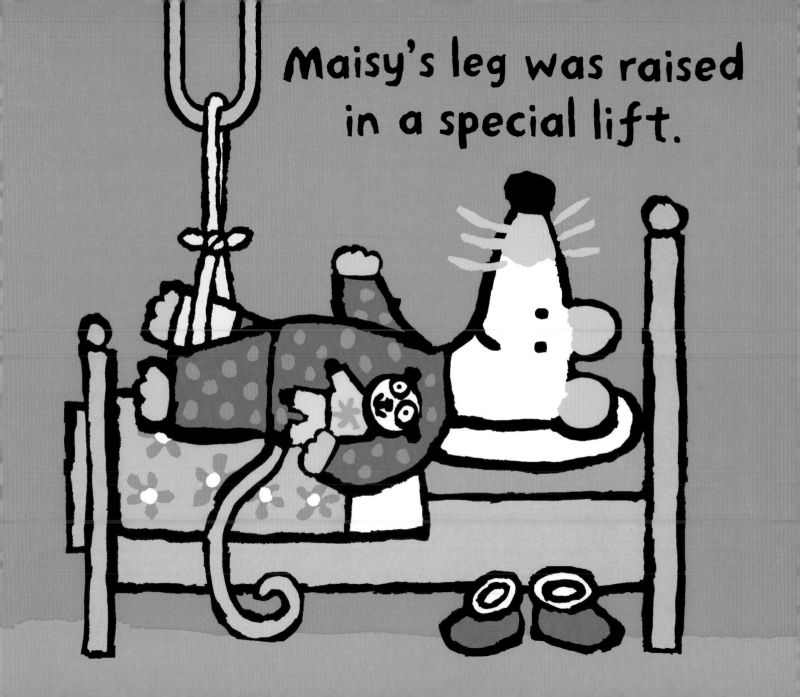

Being away from home felt strange.
Maisy missed her friends.

Tallulah and Cyril came during visiting hours the next morning.

Maisy shared her balloons and cookies with Dotty.

Before she left,
Tallulah signed
Maisy's cast.

Doctor Duck told Maisy, "You can go home now. But no trampolining yet! Come back in a few weeks to have the cast taken off."

Before Maisy left,
Nurse Comfort showed
her how to walk
using crutches.

Charley arrived to take Maisy home. "Goodbye, Dotty," Maisy said to her new friend. "Get well soon!"